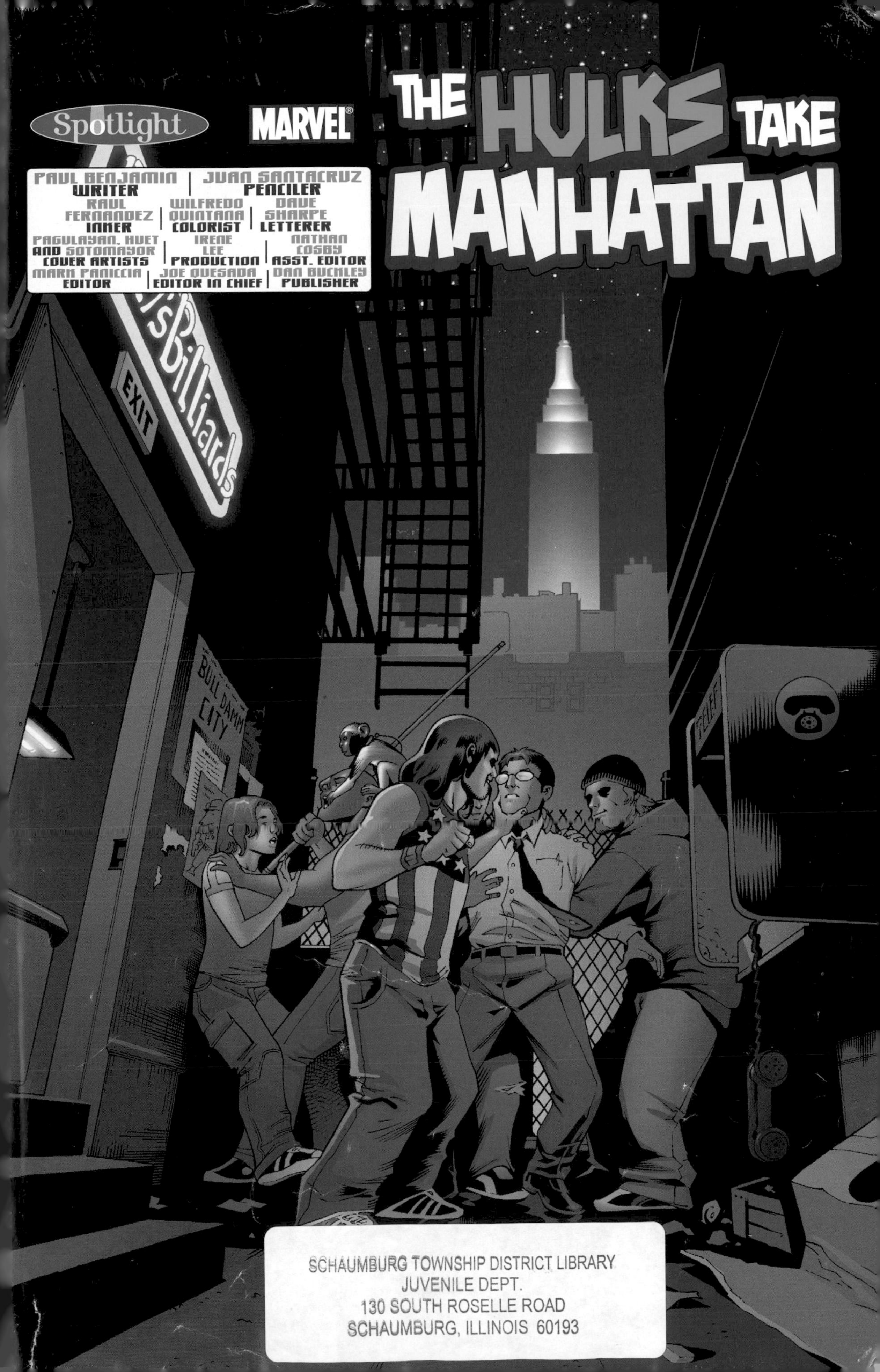
Spotlight
MARVEL
THE HULKS TAKE MANHATTAN
PAUL BENJAMIN WRITER
JUAN SANTACRUZ PENCILER
RAUL FERNANDEZ INKER
WILFREDO QUINTANA COLORIST
DAVE SHARPE LETTERER
PAGULAYAN, HUET AND SOTOMAYOR COVER ARTISTS
IRENE LEE PRODUCTION
NATHAN COSBY ASST. EDITOR
MARK PANICCIA EDITOR
JOE QUESADA EDITOR IN CHIEF
DAN BUCKLEY PUBLISHER
Billiards
EXIT
BULL DAMM CITY

3 1257 01882 7815

VISIT US AT
www.abdopublishing.com

Reinforced library bound edition published in 2009 by Spotlight, a division of the ABDO Publishing Group, 8000 West 78th Street, Edina, Minnesota 55439. Spotlight produces high-quality reinforced library bound editions for schools and libraries. Published by agreement with Marvel Characters, Inc.

Library of Congress Cataloging-in-Publication Data

Benjamin, Paul, 1970-
  The hulks take Manhattan / Paul Benjamin, writer ; Juan Santacruz, penciler ; Raul Fernandez, inker ; Wilfredo Quintana, colorist ; Dave Sharpe, letterer. -- Reinforced library bound ed.
     p. cm. -- (Hulk)
  ISBN 978-1-59961-546-2
  1. Graphic novels. [1. Graphic novels.] I. Santacruz, Juan, ill. II. Title.
  PZ7.7.B45Hul 2008
  [E]--dc22
                                                        2008000102

All Spotlight books have reinforced library bindings and are manufactured in the United States of America.

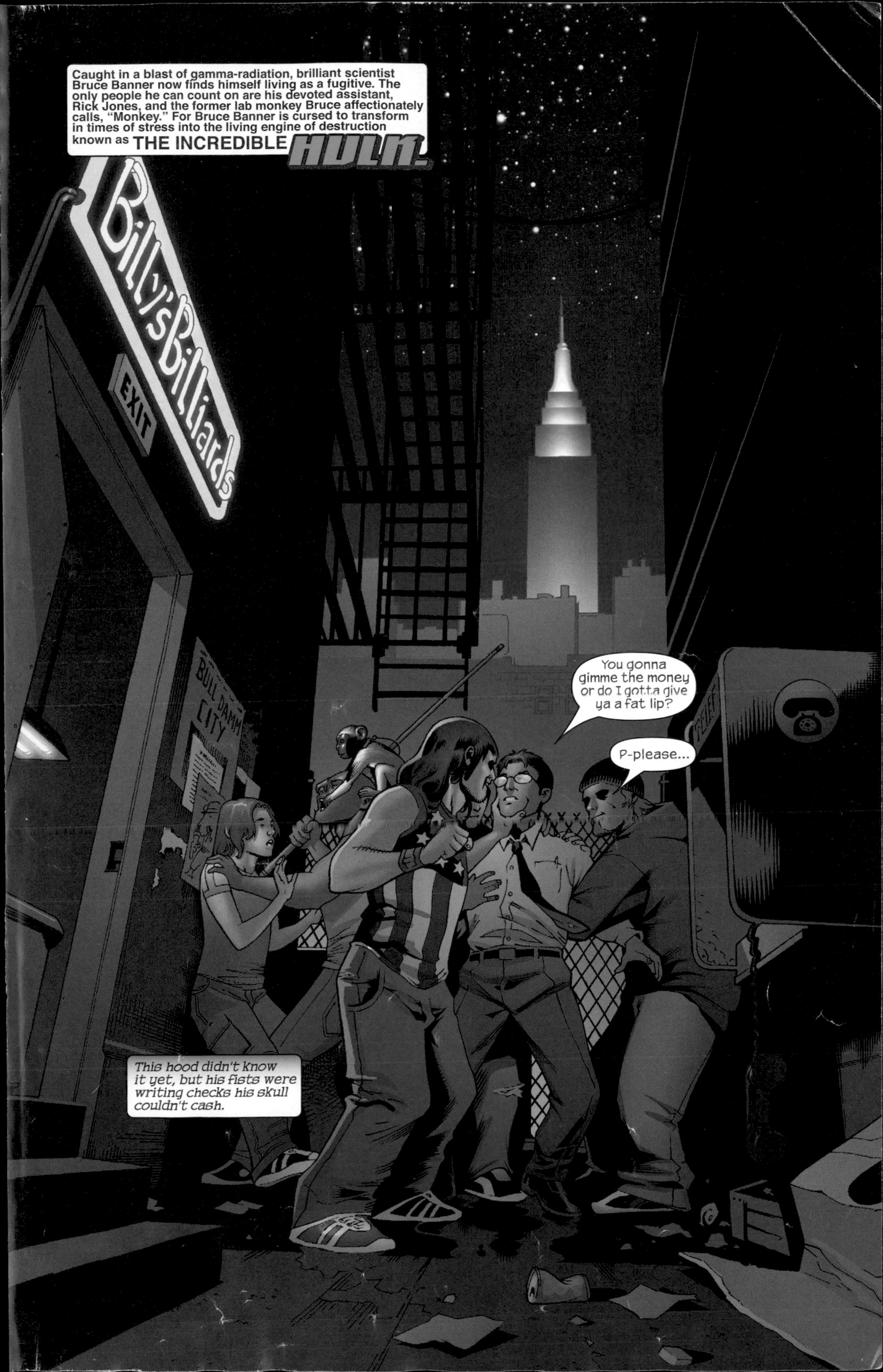
Caught in a blast of gamma-radiation, brilliant scientist Bruce Banner now finds himself living as a fugitive. The only people he can count on are his devoted assistant, Rick Jones, and the former lab monkey Bruce affectionately calls, "Monkey." For Bruce Banner is cursed to transform in times of stress into the living engine of destruction known as THE INCREDIBLE HULK.
Billy's Billiards
EXIT
BULL DAMM CITY
You gonna gimme the money or do I gotta give ya a fat lip?
P-please...
This hood didn't know it yet, but his fists were writing checks his skull couldn't cash.

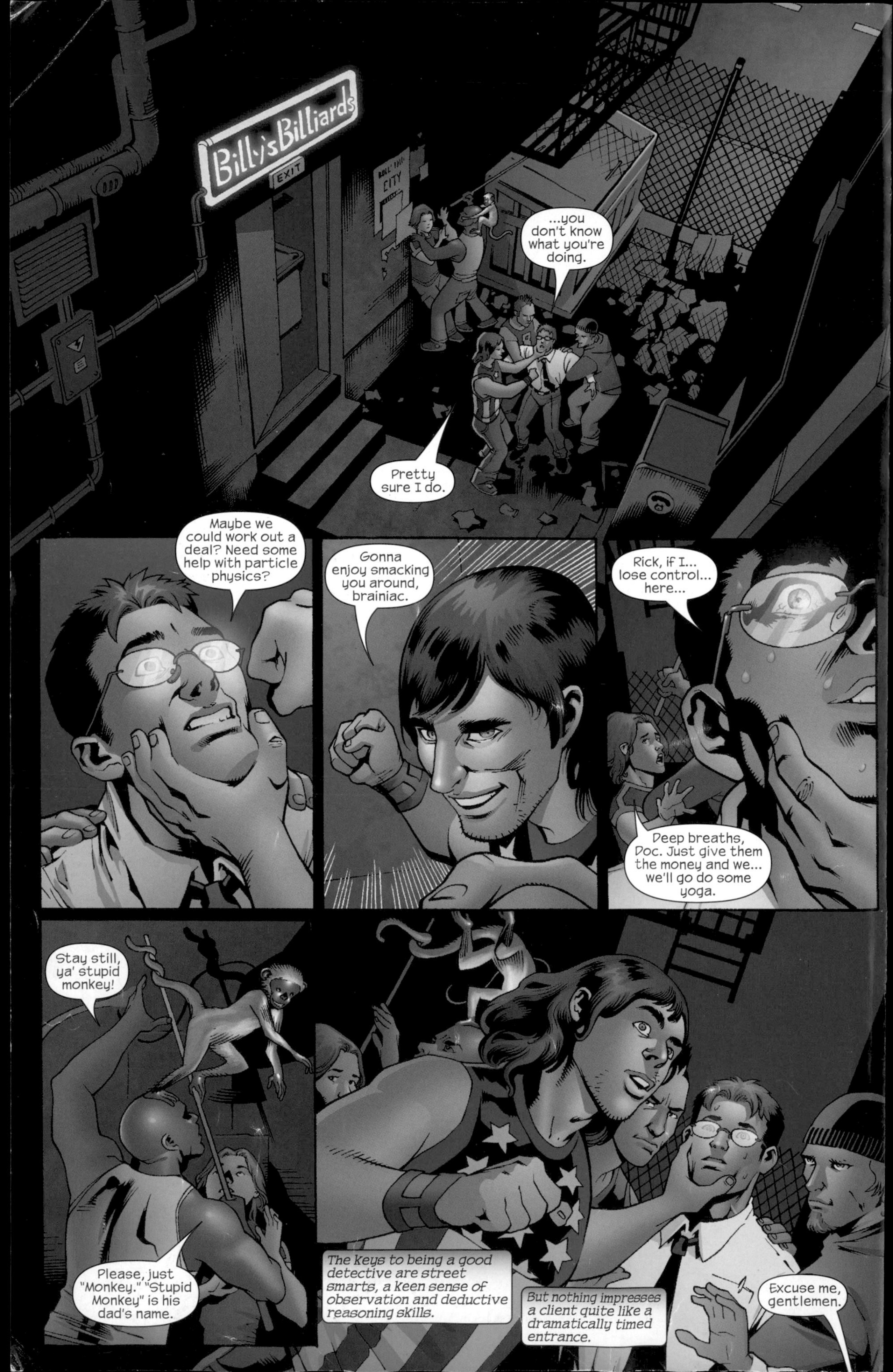
Billy's Billiards
EXIT
...you don't know what you're doing.
Pretty sure I do.
Maybe we could work out a deal? Need some help with particle physics?
Gonna enjoy smacking you around, brainiac.
Rick, if I... lose control... here...
Deep breaths, Doc. Just give them the money and we... we'll go do some yoga.
Stay still, ya' stupid monkey!
Please, just "Monkey." "Stupid Monkey" is his dad's name.
The keys to being a good detective are street smarts, a keen sense of observation and deductive reasoning skills.
But nothing impresses a client quite like a dramatically timed entrance.
Excuse me, gentlemen.

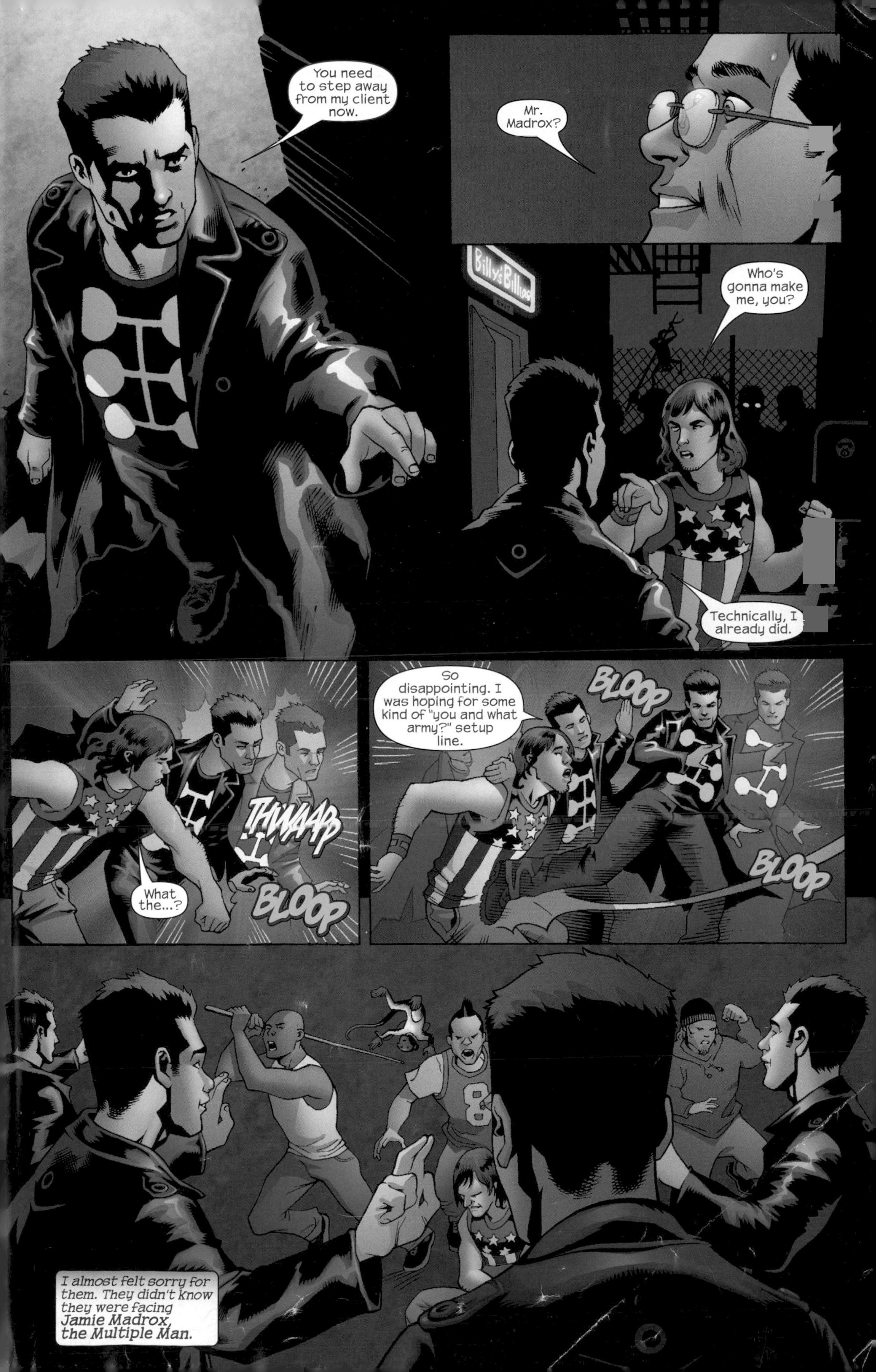
You need to step away from my client now.
Mr. Madrox?
Billy's Billiards
Who's gonna make me, you?
Technically, I already did.
THWAAPP
What the...?
BLOOP
So disappointing. I was hoping for some kind of "you and what army?" setup line.
BLOOP
BLOOP
I almost felt sorry for them. They didn't know they were facing Jamie Madrox, the Multiple Man.

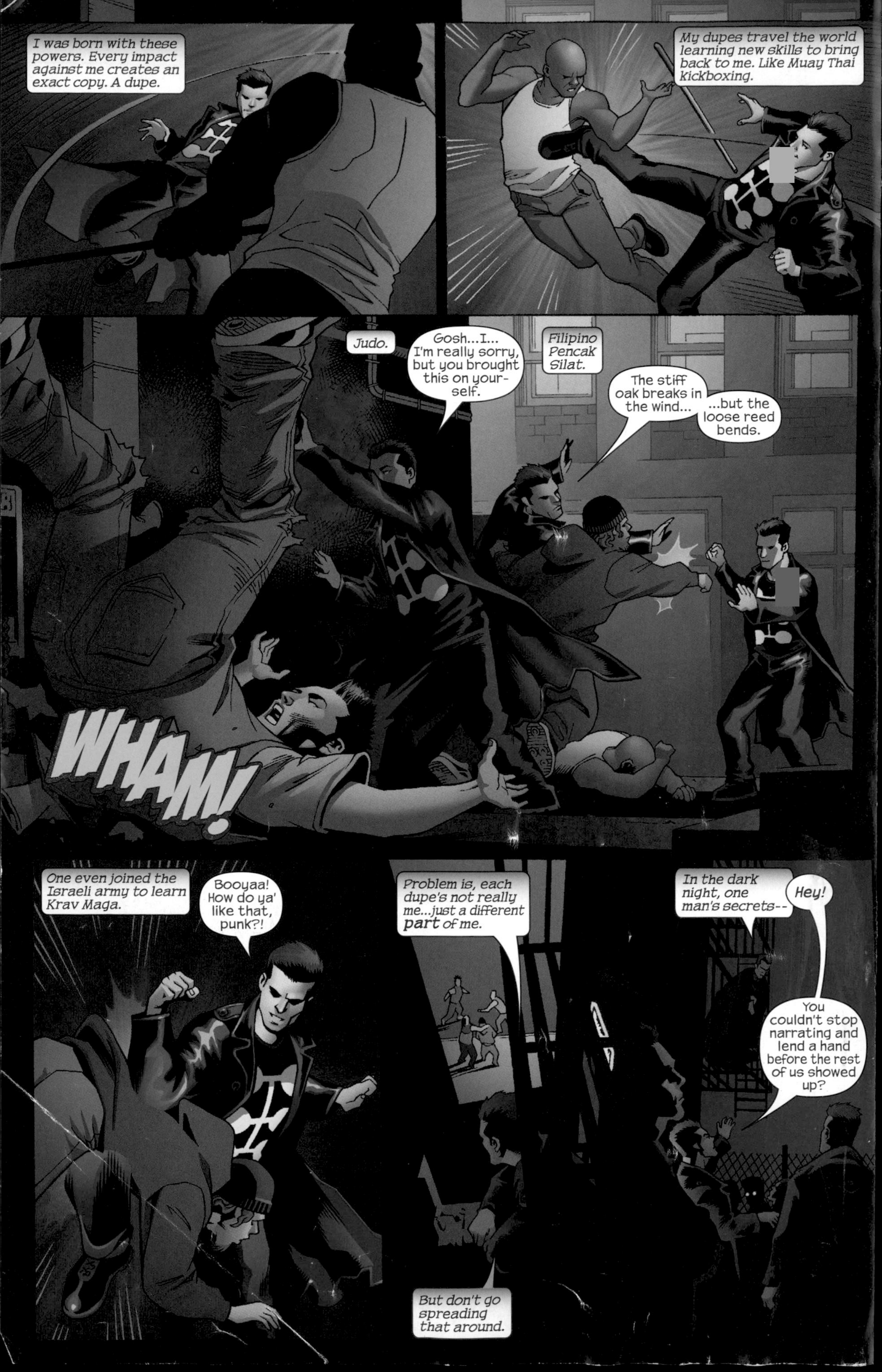

I was born with these powers. Every impact against me creates an exact copy. A dupe.
My dupes travel the world learning new skills to bring back to me. Like Muay Thai kickboxing.
Judo.
Gosh...I... I'm really sorry, but you brought this on your-self.
Filipino Pencak Silat.
The stiff oak breaks in the wind...
...but the loose reed bends.
WHAM!
One even joined the Israeli army to learn Krav Maga.
Booyaa! How do ya' like that, punk?!
Problem is, each dupe's not really me...just a different **part** of me.
But don't go spreading that around.
In the dark night, one man's secrets--
Hey!
You couldn't stop narrating and lend a hand before the rest of us showed up?

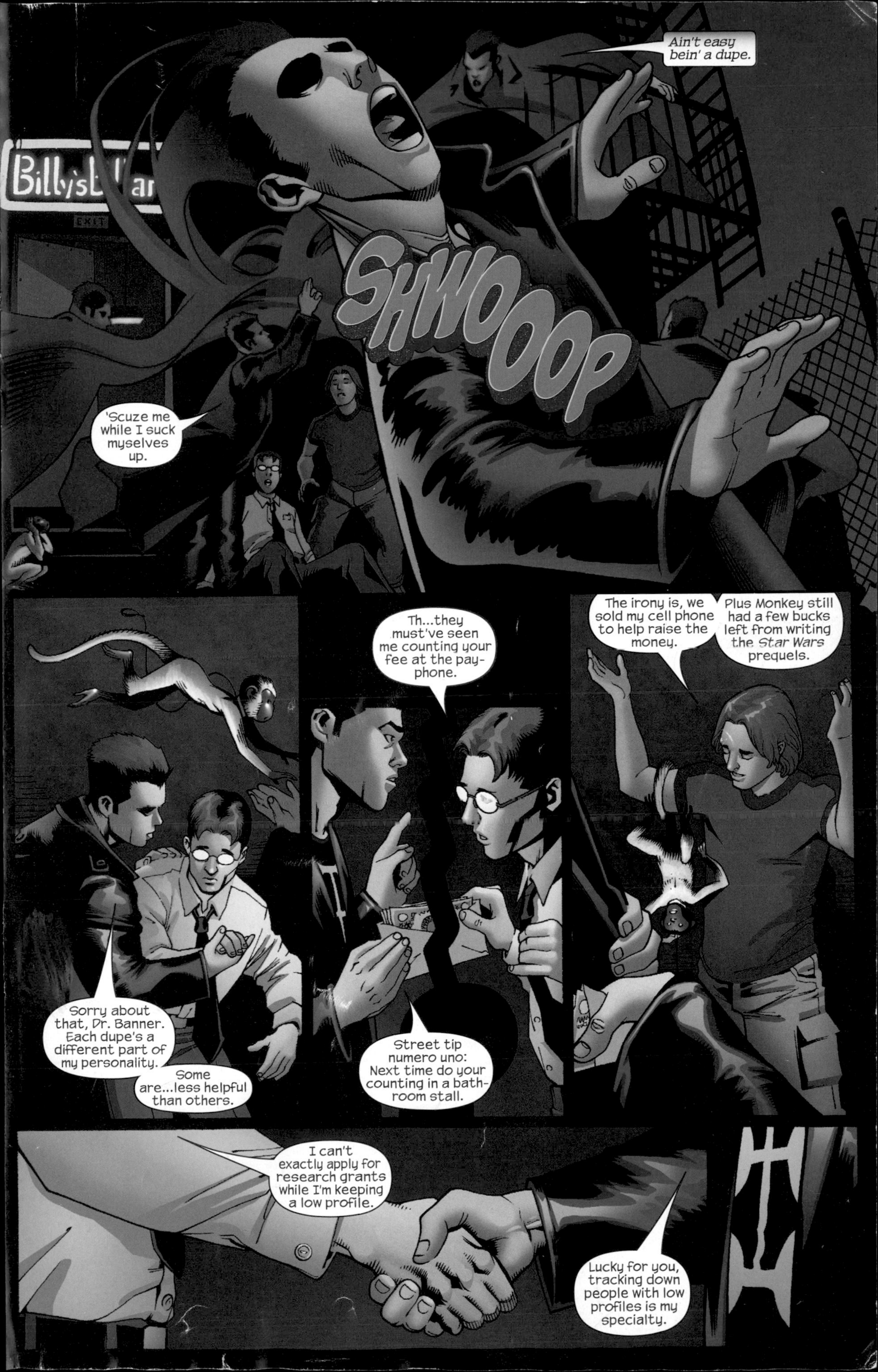
Ain't easy bein' a dupe.
Billy's B
EXIT
SHWOOOP
'Scuze me while I suck myselves up.
Sorry about that, Dr. Banner. Each dupe's a different part of my personality.
Some are...less helpful than others.
Th...they must've seen me counting your fee at the pay-phone.
Street tip numero uno: Next time do your counting in a bath-room stall.
The irony is, we sold my cell phone to help raise the money.
Plus Monkey still had a few bucks left from writing the *Star Wars* prequels.
I can't exactly apply for research grants while I'm keeping a low profile.
Lucky for you, tracking down people with low profiles is my specialty.

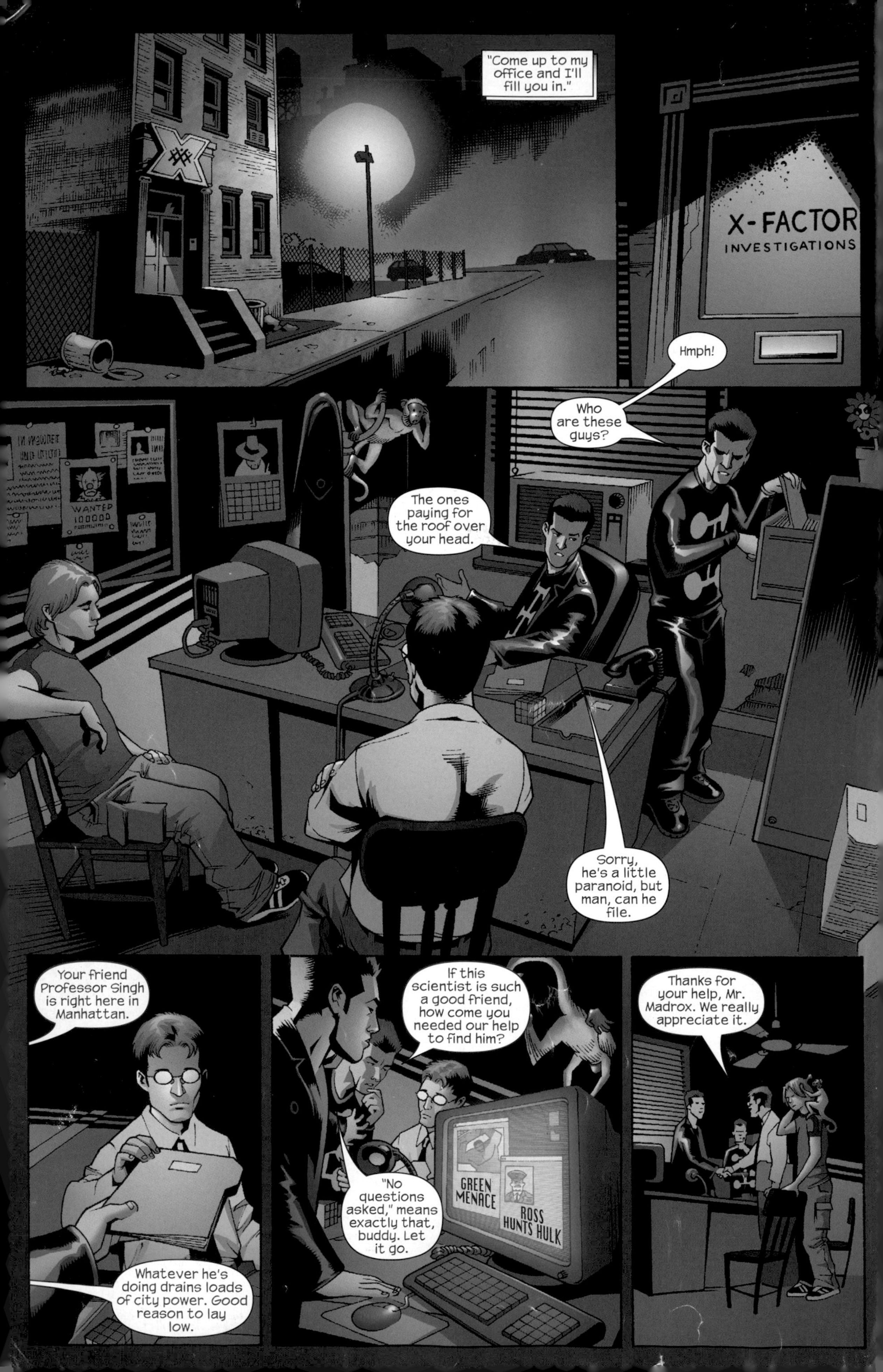
"Come up to my office and I'll fill you in."
X-FACTOR INVESTIGATIONS
Hmph!
Who are these guys?
The ones paying for the roof over your head.
Sorry, he's a little paranoid, but man, can he file.
WANTED
Your friend Professor Singh is right here in Manhattan.
Whatever he's doing drains loads of city power. Good reason to lay low.
If this scientist is such a good friend, how come you needed our help to find him?
"No questions asked," means exactly that, buddy. Let it go.
GREEN MENACE
ROSS HUNTS HULK
Thanks for your help, Mr. Madrox. We really appreciate it.

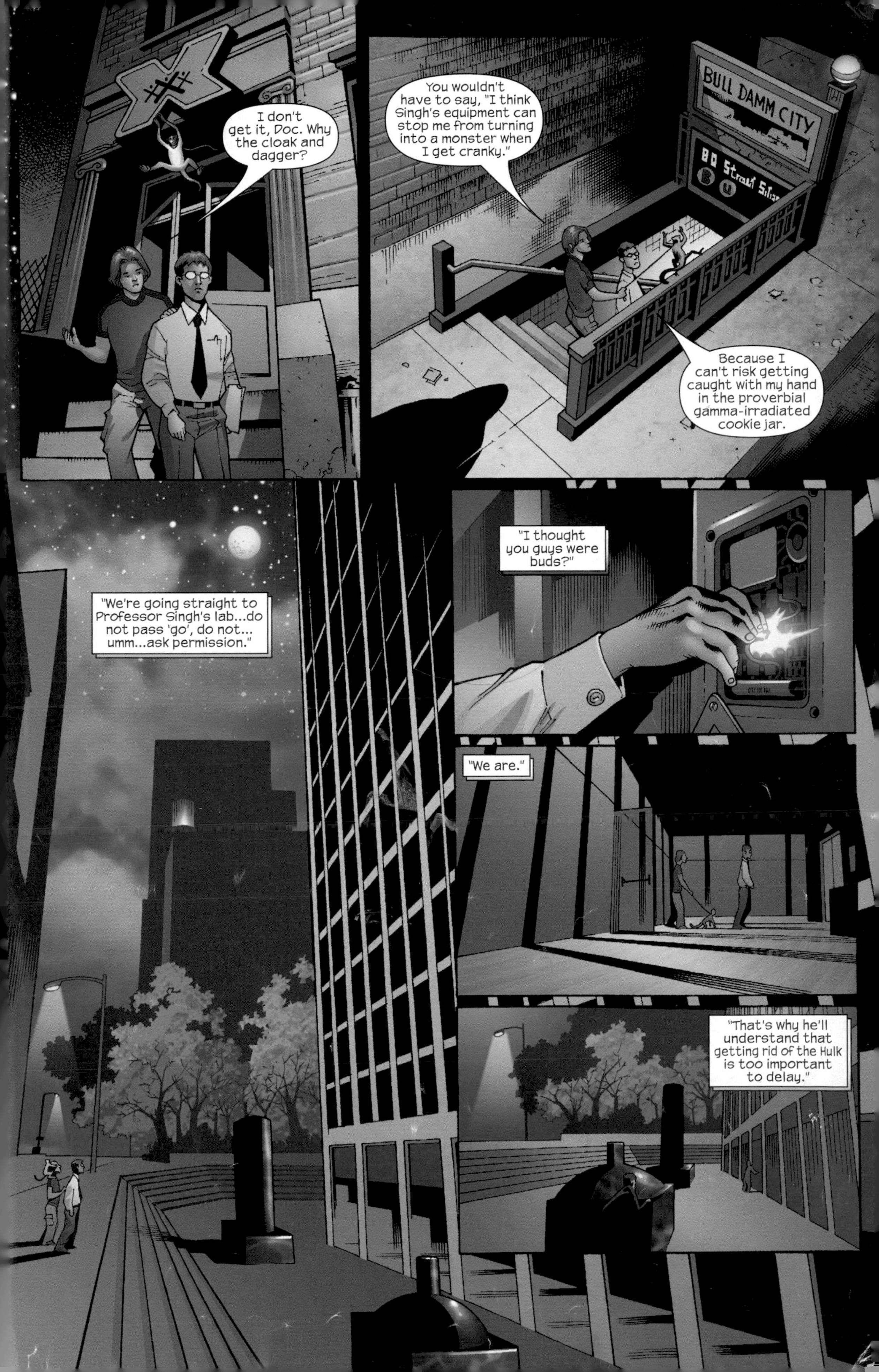
I don't get it, Doc. Why the cloak and dagger?
You wouldn't have to say, "I think Singh's equipment can stop me from turning into a monster when I get cranky."
BULL DAMM CITY
Because I can't risk getting caught with my hand in the proverbial gamma-irradiated cookie jar.
"We're going straight to Professor Singh's lab...do not pass 'go', do not... umm...ask permission."
"I thought you guys were buds?"
"We are."
"That's why he'll understand that getting rid of the Hulk is too important to delay."

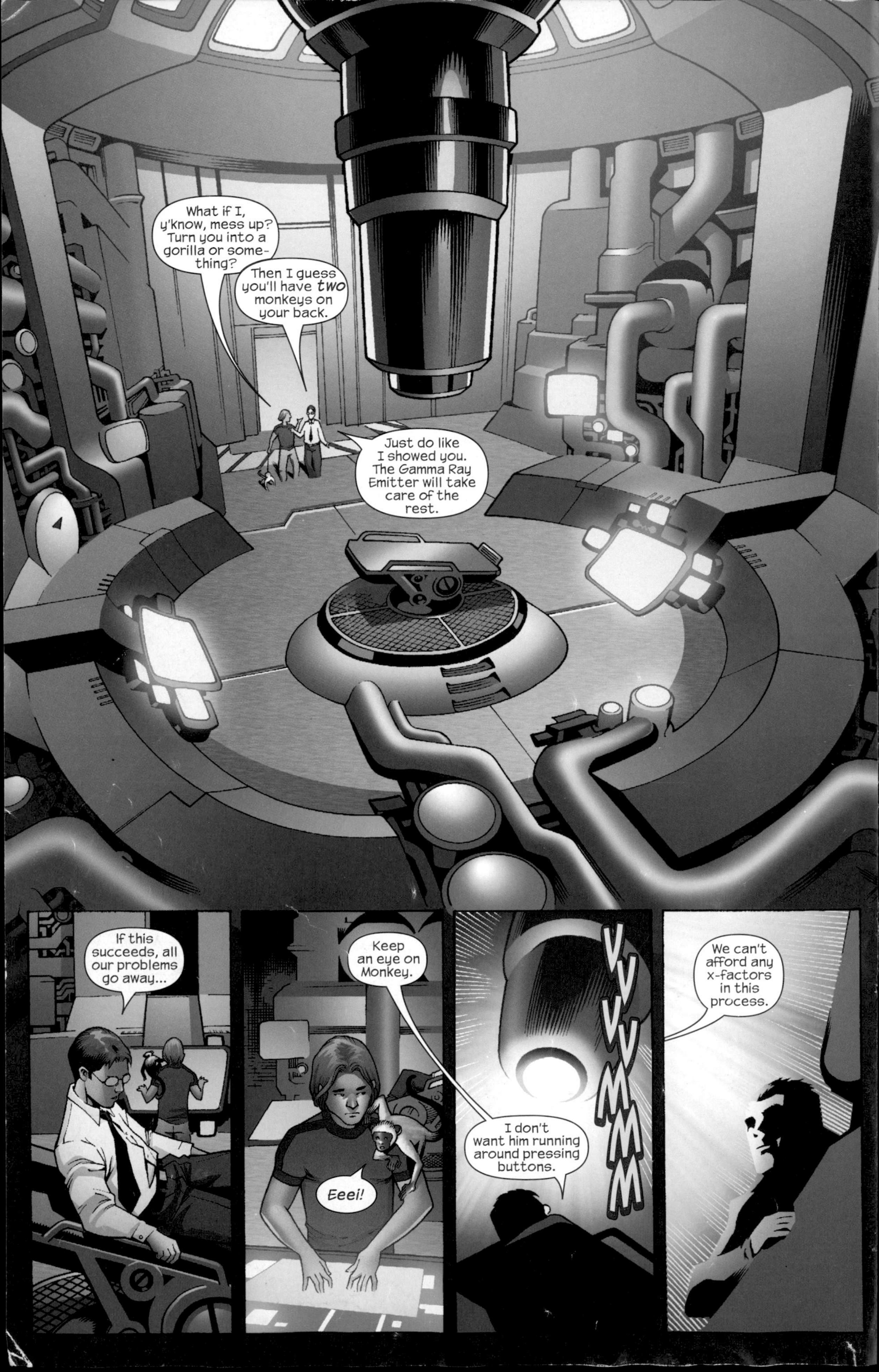
What if I, y'know, mess up? Turn you into a gorilla or some-thing?
Then I guess you'll have *two* monkeys on your back.
Just do like I showed you. The Gamma Ray Emitter will take care of the rest.
If this succeeds, all our problems go away...
Keep an eye on Monkey.
Eeei!
I don't want him running around pressing buttons.
VVVVMMMM
We can't afford any x-factors in this process.

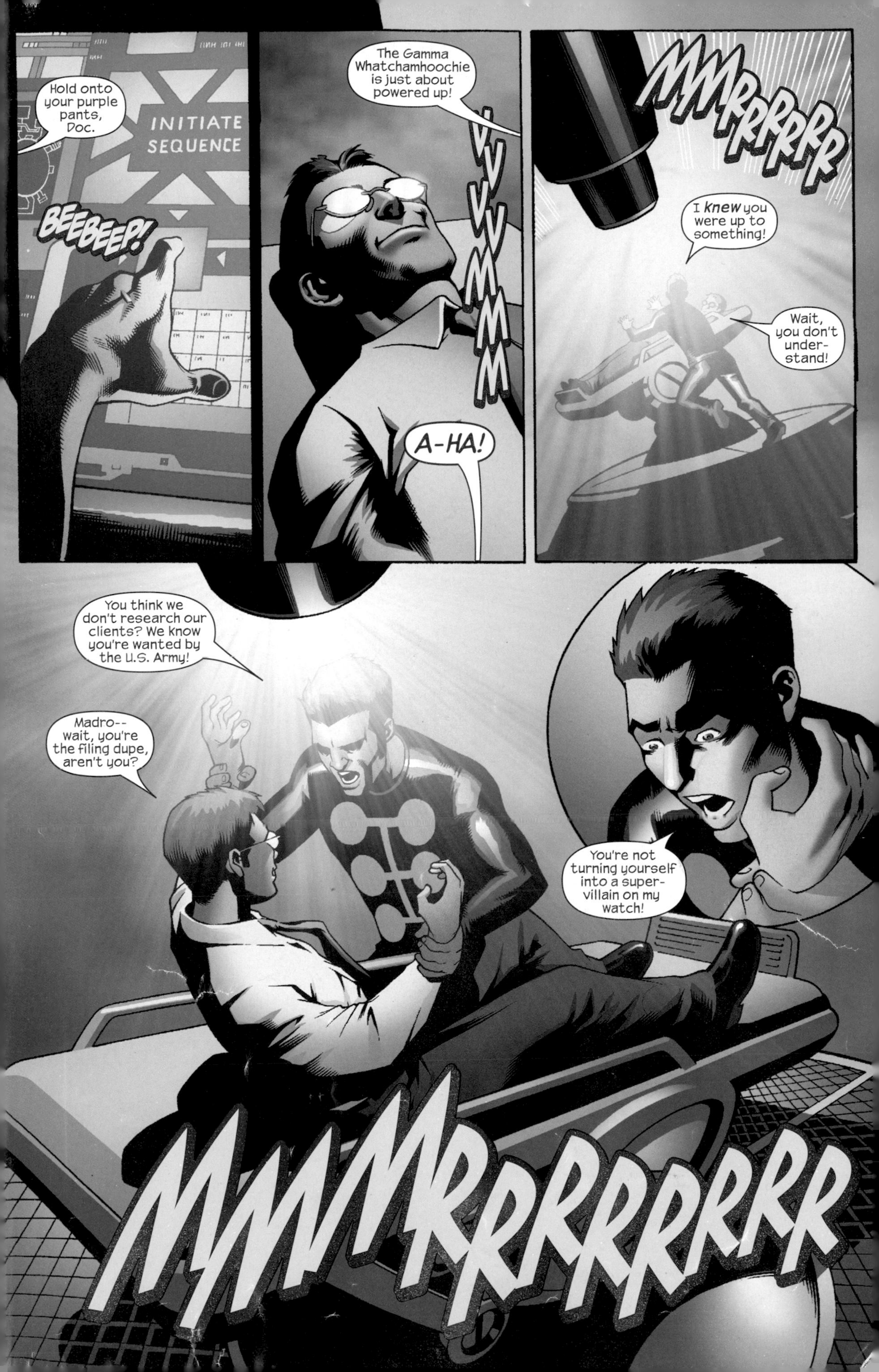
Hold onto your purple pants, Doc.
INITIATE SEQUENCE
BEEBEEP!
The Gamma Whatchamhoochie is just about powered up!
VVVVMMMM
A-HA!
MMRRRRRR
I knew you were up to something!
Wait, you don't under-stand!
You think we don't research our clients? We know you're wanted by the U.S. Army!
Madro-- wait, you're the filing dupe, aren't you?
You're not turning yourself into a super-villain on my watch!
MMMRRRRRRRRR

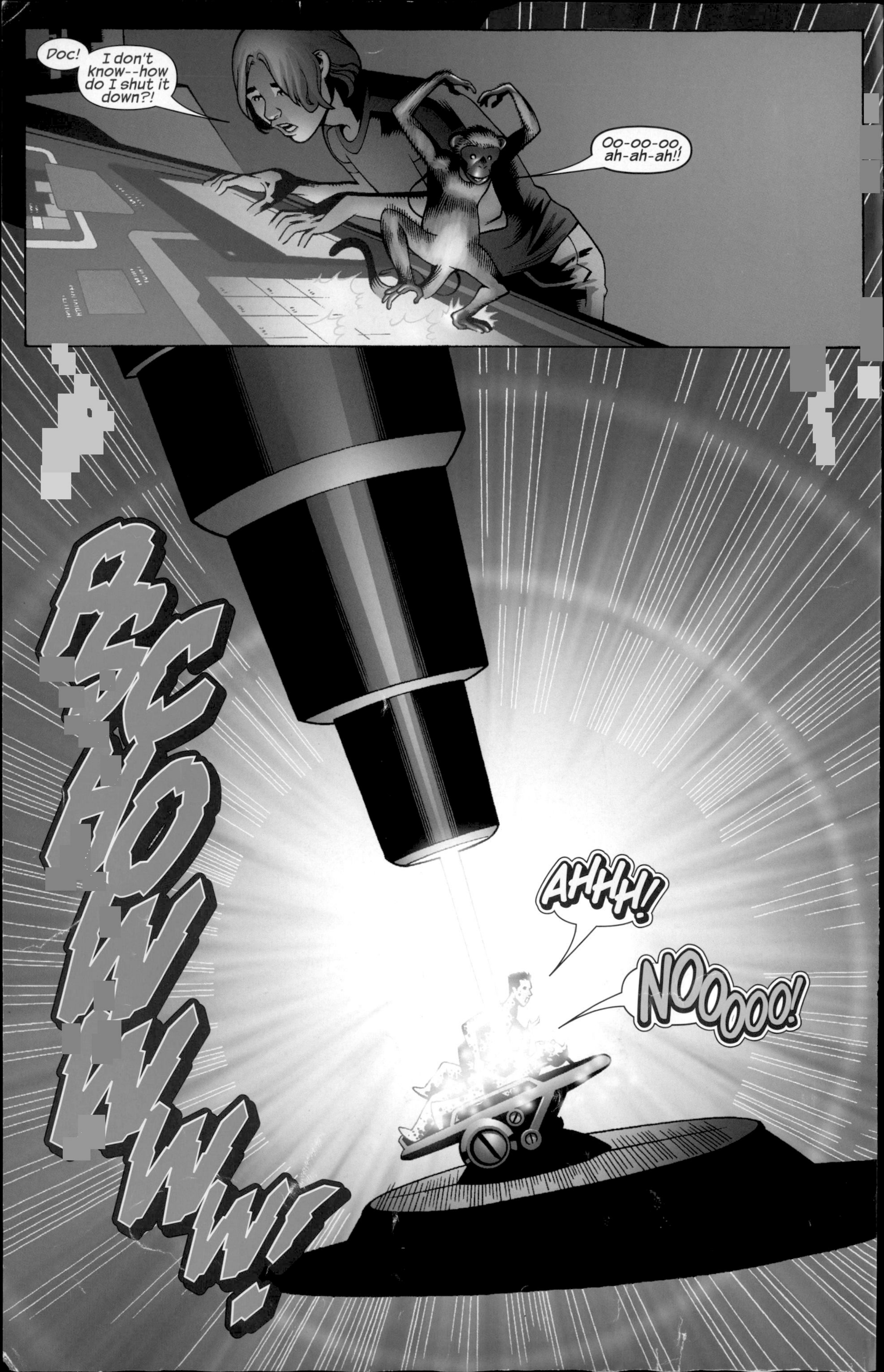
Doc!
I don't know--how do I shut it down?!
Oo-oo-oo, ah-ah-ah!!
AHHH!!
NOOOOOO!

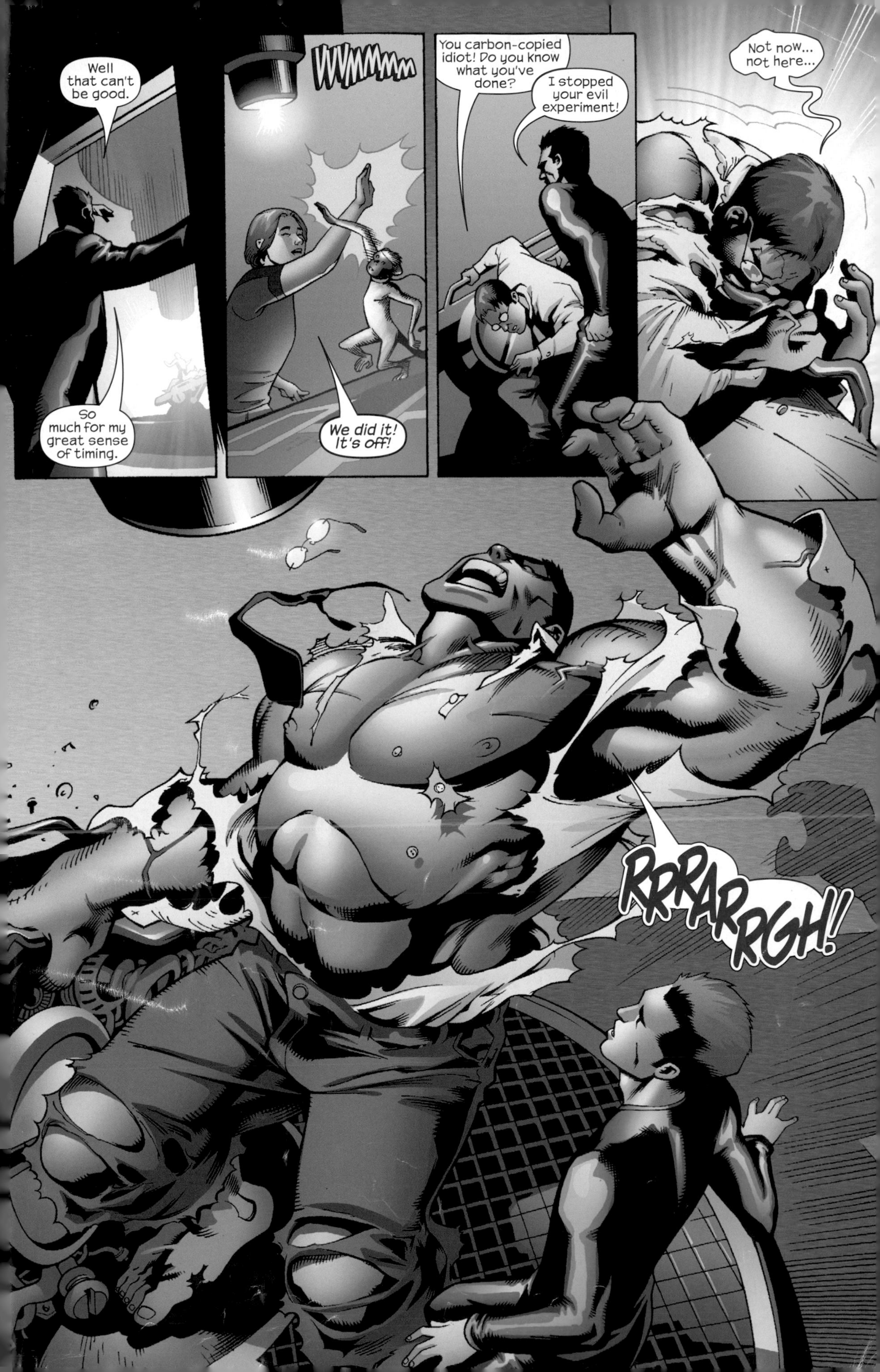
Well that can't be good.
So much for my great sense of timing.
VVVMMMmm
We did it! It's off!
You carbon-copied idiot! Do you know what you've done?
I stopped your evil experiment!
Not now... not here...
RRRARRRGH!

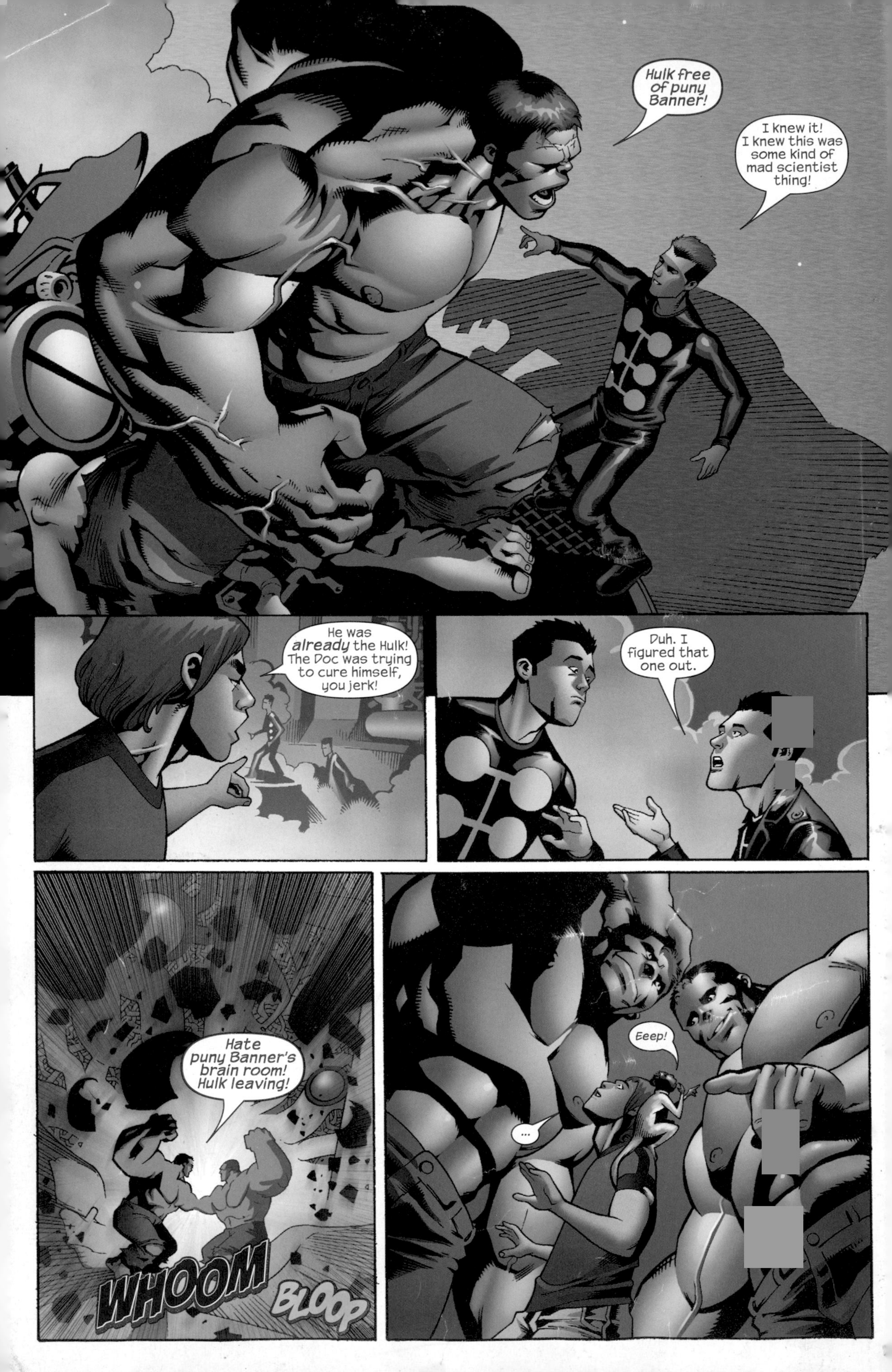
Hulk free of puny Banner!
I knew it! I knew this was some kind of mad scientist thing!
He was *already* the Hulk! The Doc was trying to cure himself, you jerk!
Duh. I figured that one out.
Hate puny Banner's brain room! Hulk leaving!
WHOOM
BLOOP
...
Eeep!

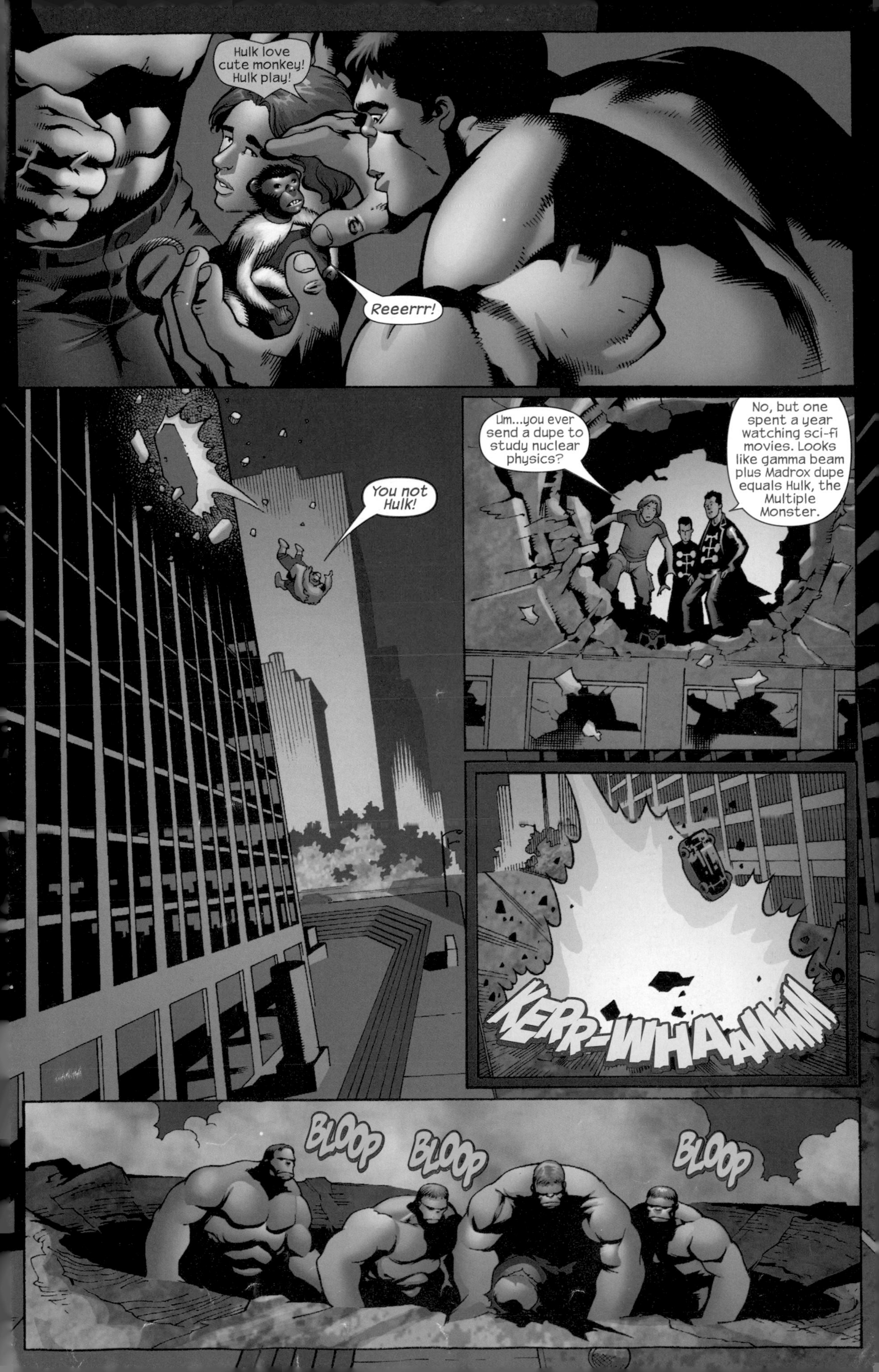
Hulk love cute monkey! Hulk play!
Reeerrr!
You not Hulk!
Um...you ever send a dupe to study nuclear physics?
No, but one spent a year watching sci-fi movies. Looks like gamma beam plus Madrox dupe equals Hulk, the Multiple Monster.
KERR-WHAAMM
BLOOP
BLOOP
BLOOP

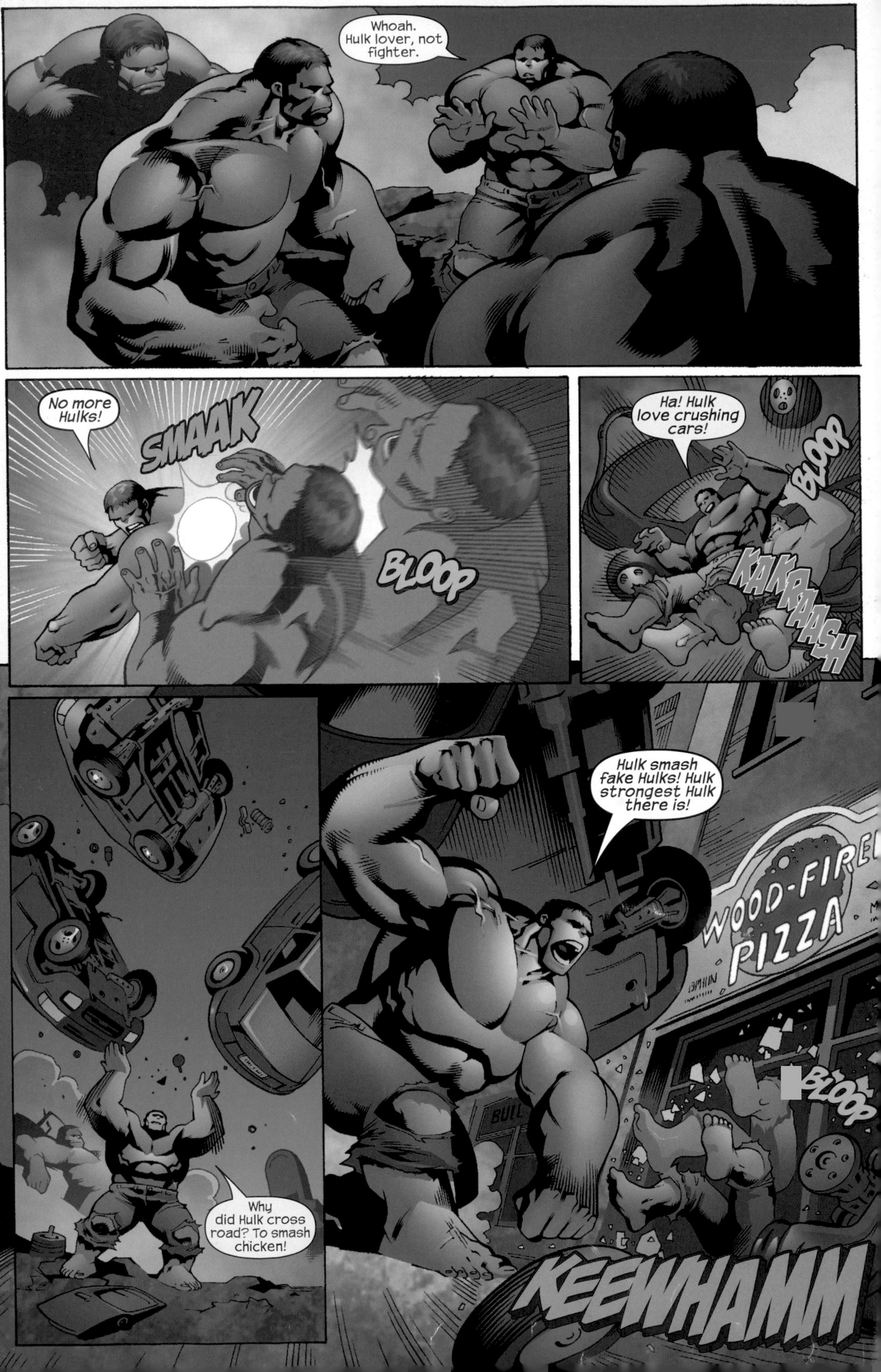

Whoah. Hulk lover, not fighter.
No more Hulks!
SMAAK
BLOOP
Ha! Hulk love crushing cars!
BLOOP
KAKRAASH
Hulk smash fake Hulks! Hulk strongest Hulk there is!
WOOD-FIRE
PIZZA
BLOOP
Why did Hulk cross road? To smash chicken!
KEEWHAMM

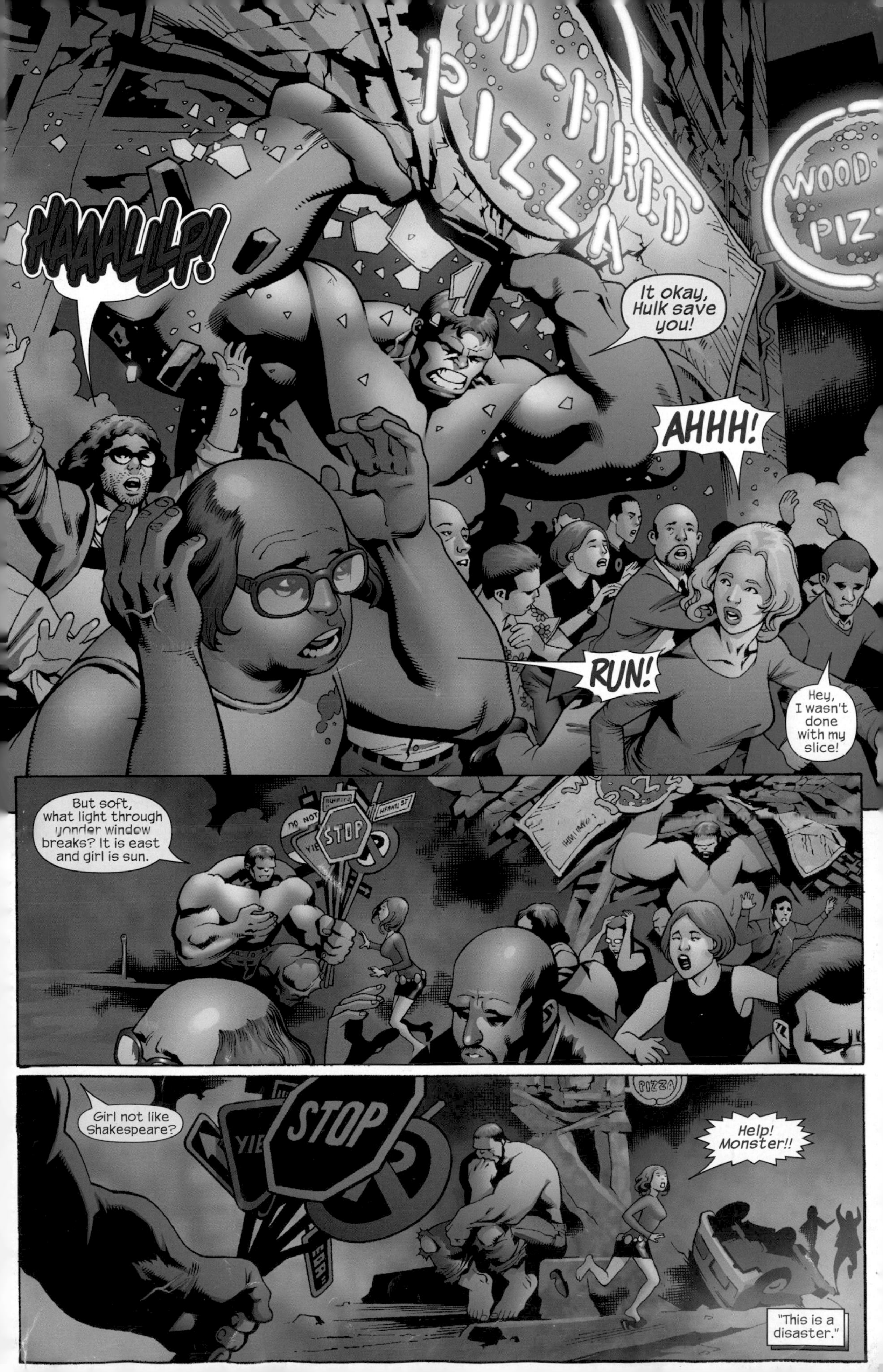

WOOD-FIRED PIZZA
WOOD-PIZZ
HAAALLLP!
It okay, Hulk save you!
AHHH!
RUN!
Hey, I wasn't done with my slice!
But soft, what light through yonder window breaks? It is east and girl is sun.
STOP
Girl not like Shakespeare?
STOP
PIZZA
Help! Monster!!
"This is a disaster."

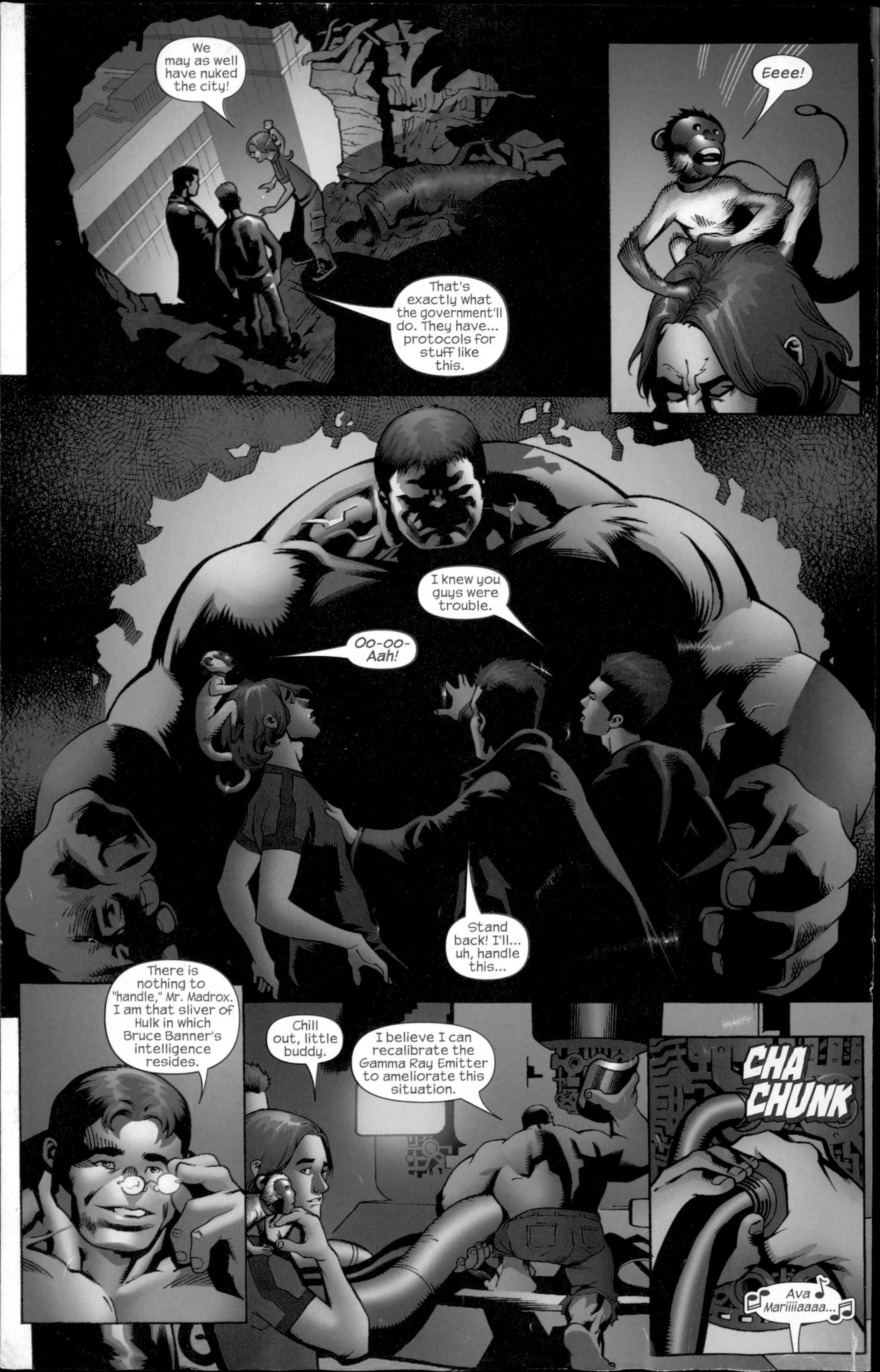
We may as well have nuked the city!
That's exactly what the government'll do. They have... protocols for stuff like this.
Eeee!
I knew you guys were trouble.
Oo-oo-Aah!
Stand back! I'll... uh, handle this...
There is nothing to "handle," Mr. Madrox. I am that sliver of Hulk in which Bruce Banner's intelligence resides.
Chill out, little buddy.
I believe I can recalibrate the Gamma Ray Emitter to ameliorate this situation.
CHA CHUNK
Ava Mariiiiaaaa...

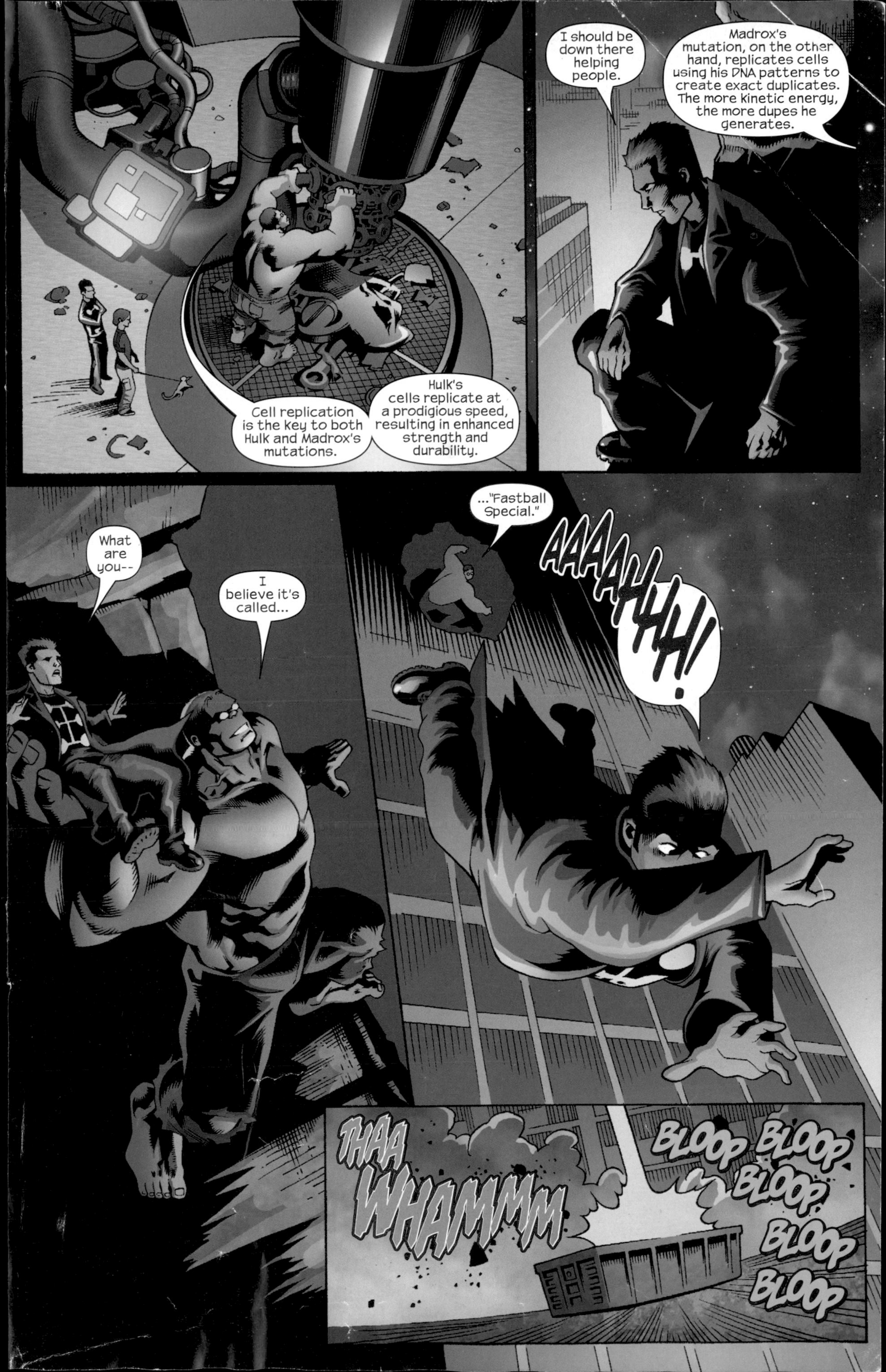
Cell replication is the key to both Hulk and Madrox's mutations.
Hulk's cells replicate at a prodigious speed, resulting in enhanced strength and durability.
I should be down there helping people.
Madrox's mutation, on the other hand, replicates cells using his DNA patterns to create exact duplicates. The more kinetic energy, the more dupes he generates.
What are you--
I believe it's called...
..."Fastball Special."
AAAAHHH!
THAA WHAMMM
BLOOP BLOOP BLOOP BLOOP BLOOP

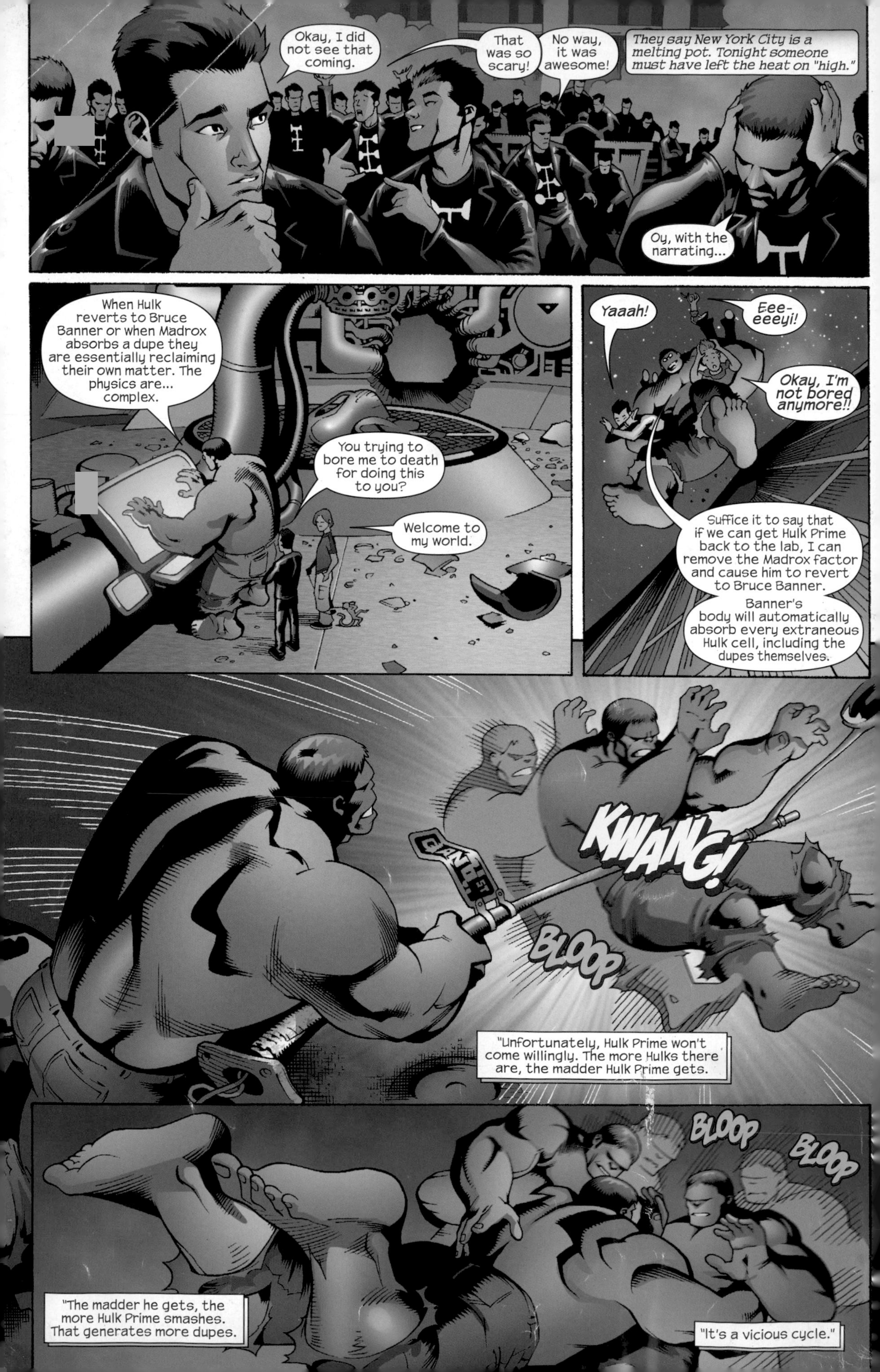

Okay, I did not see that coming.
That was so scary!
No way, it was awesome!
They say New York City is a melting pot. Tonight someone must have left the heat on "high."
Oy, with the narrating...
When Hulk reverts to Bruce Banner or when Madrox absorbs a dupe they are essentially reclaiming their own matter. The physics are... complex.
You trying to bore me to death for doing this to you?
Welcome to my world.
Yaaah!
Eee-eeeyi!
Okay, I'm not bored anymore!!
Suffice it to say that if we can get Hulk Prime back to the lab, I can remove the Madrox factor and cause him to revert to Bruce Banner.
Banner's body will automatically absorb every extraneous Hulk cell, including the dupes themselves.
KWANG!
BLOOP
"Unfortunately, Hulk Prime won't come willingly. The more Hulks there are, the madder Hulk Prime gets.
BLOOP
BLOOP
"The madder he gets, the more Hulk Prime smashes. That generates more dupes.
"It's a vicious cycle."

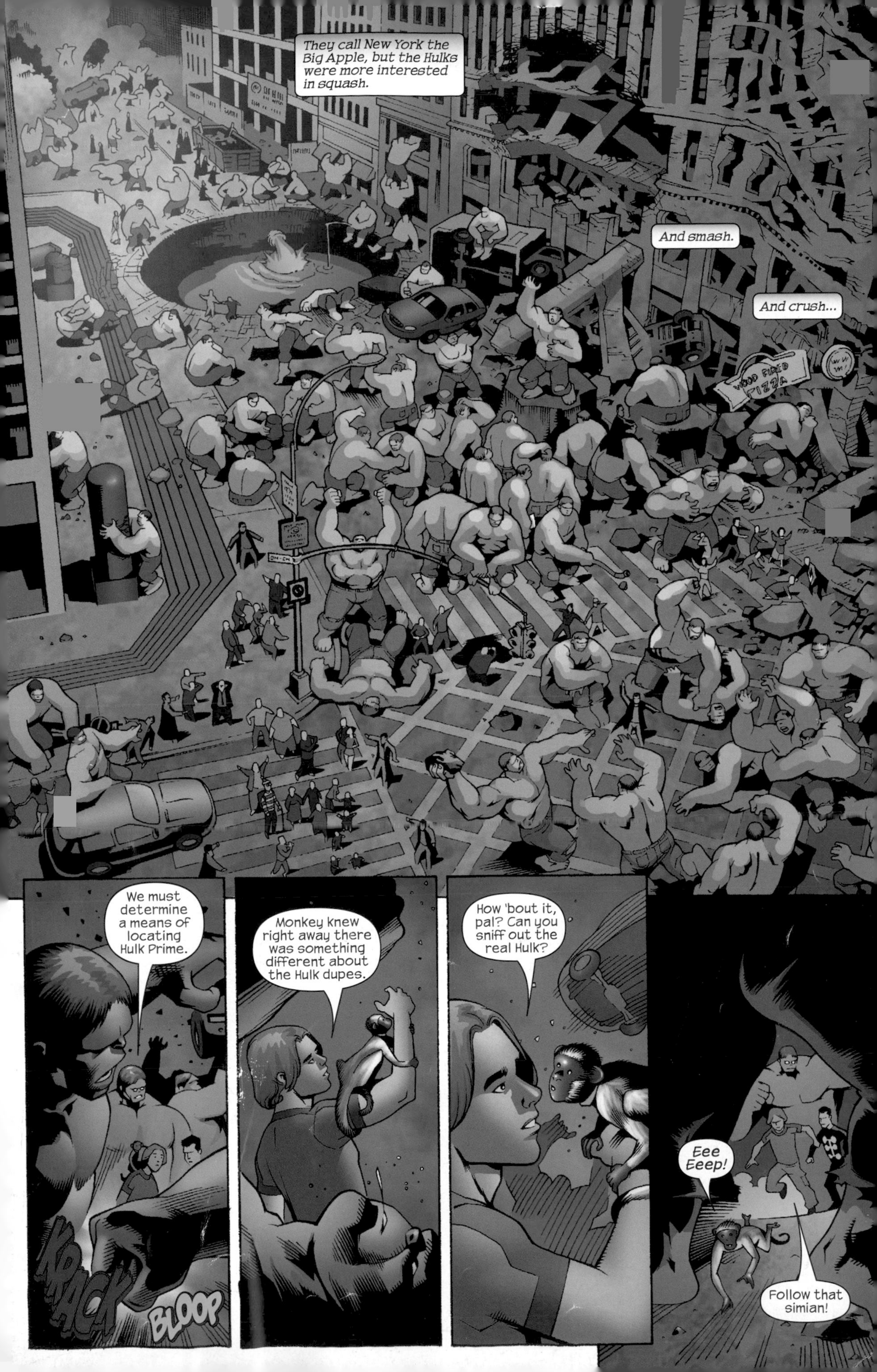
They call New York the Big Apple, but the Hulks were more interested in squash.
And smash.
And crush...
WOOD FIRED PIZZA
We must determine a means of locating Hulk Prime.
KRACK
BLOOP
Monkey knew right away there was something different about the Hulk dupes.
How 'bout it, pal? Can you sniff out the real Hulk?
Eee Eeep!
Follow that simian!

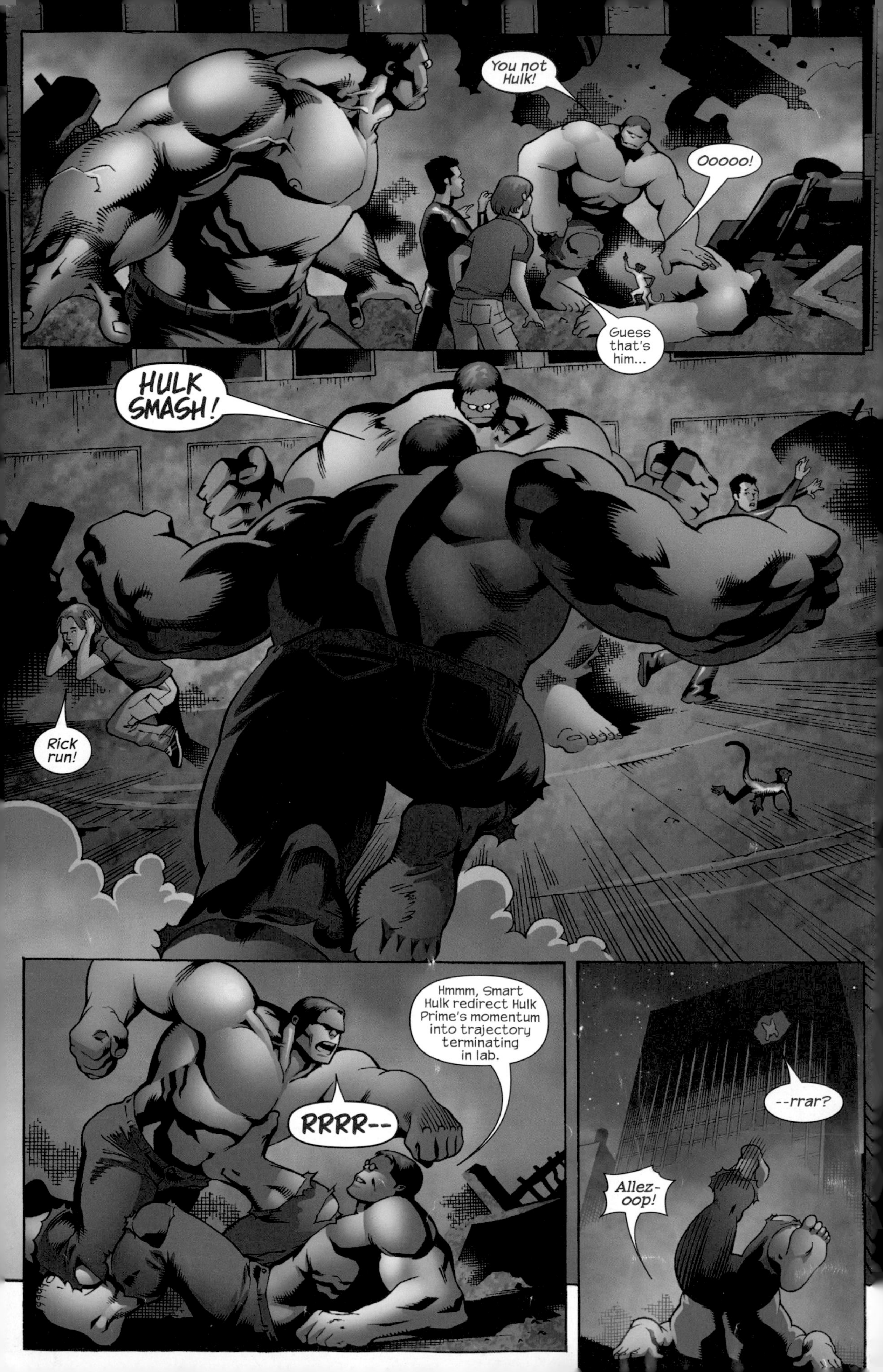
You not Hulk!
Ooooo!
Guess that's him...
HULK SMASH!
Rick run!
Hmmm, Smart Hulk redirect Hulk Prime's momentum into trajectory terminating in lab.
RRRR--
--rrar?
Allez-oop!

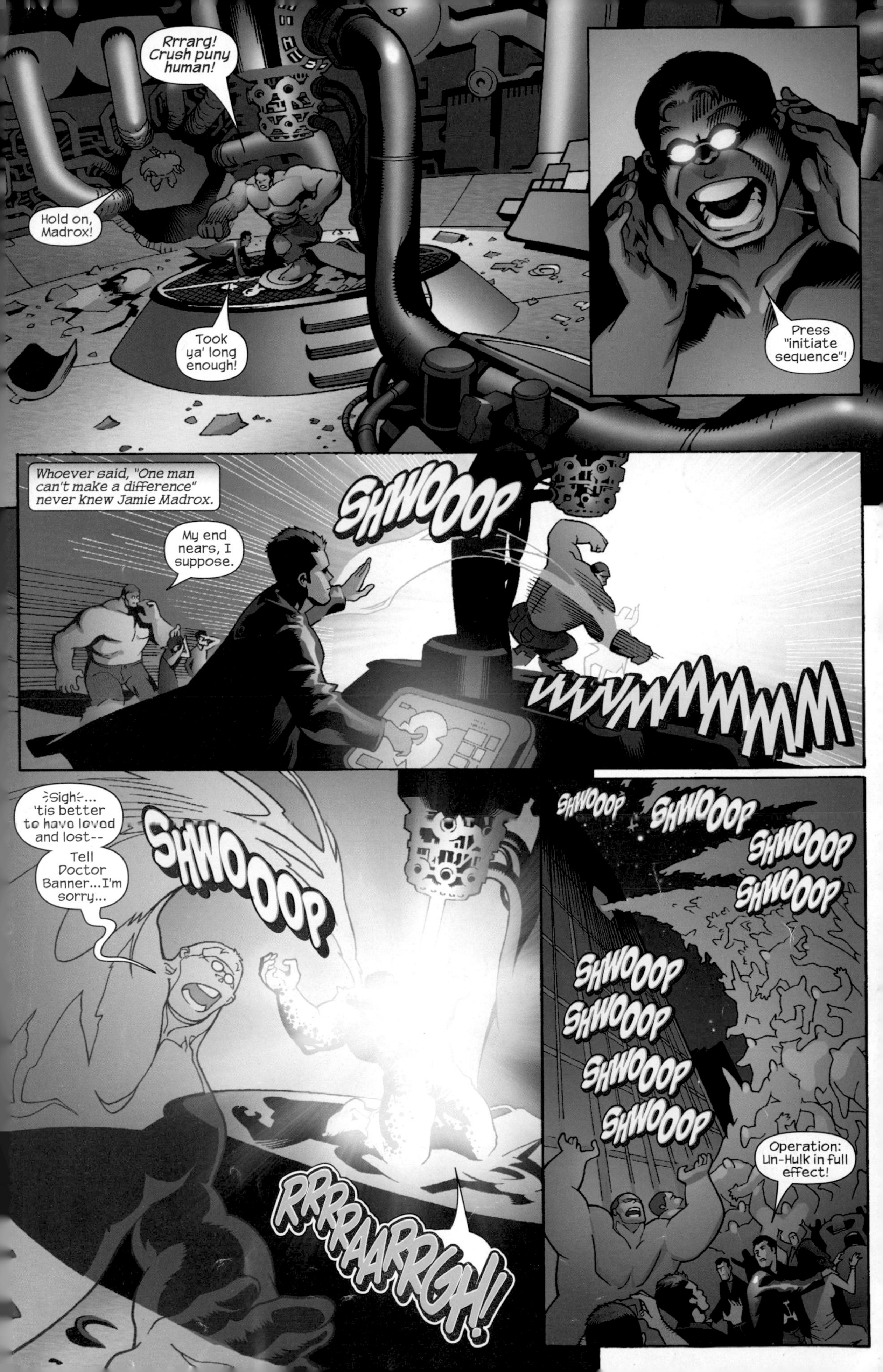
Rrrarg! Crush puny human!
Hold on, Madrox!
Took ya' long enough!
Press "initiate sequence"!
Whoever said, "One man can't make a difference" never knew Jamie Madrox.
SHWOOOP
My end nears, I suppose.
WWVMMMMMM
Sigh... 'tis better to have loved and lost--
SHWOOOP
Tell Doctor Banner...I'm sorry...
RRRRAARRGH!
SHWOOOP
SHWOOOP
SHWOOOP
SHWOOOP
SHWOOOP
SHWOOOP
SHWOOOP
SHWOOOP
Operation: Un-Hulk in full effect!

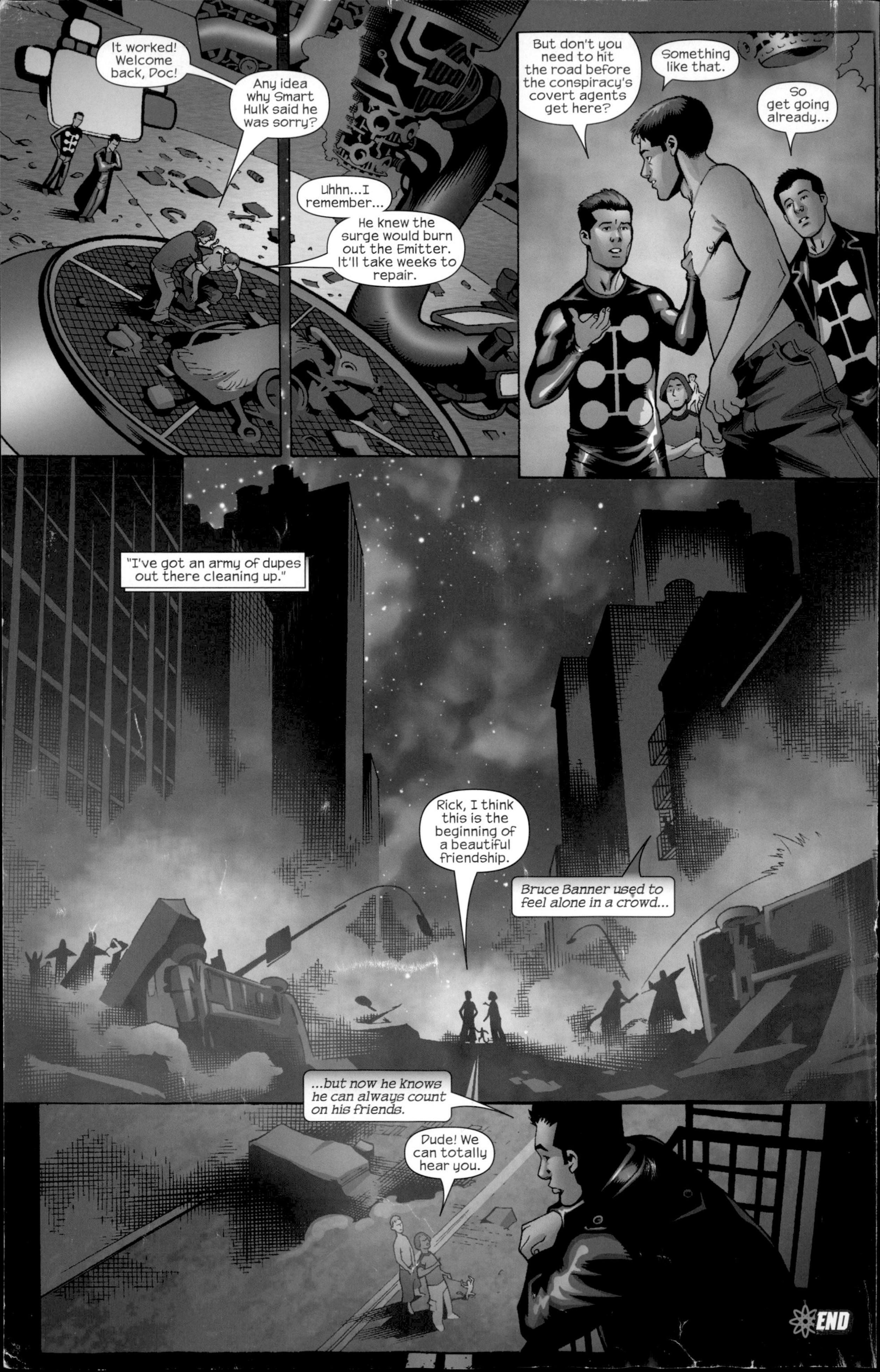
It worked! Welcome back, Doc!
Any idea why Smart Hulk said he was sorry?
Uhhn...I remember...
He knew the surge would burn out the Emitter. It'll take weeks to repair.
But don't you need to hit the road before the conspiracy's covert agents get here?
Something like that.
So get going already...
"I've got an army of dupes out there cleaning up."
Rick, I think this is the beginning of a beautiful friendship.
Bruce Banner used to feel alone in a crowd...
...but now he knows he can always count on his friends.
Dude! We can totally hear you.
END